Anonymous

Counsels on Spiritualism

Anatiposi

Anonymous

Counsels on Spiritualism

Reprint of the original.

1st Edition 2023 | ISBN: 978-3-38230-850-6

Anatiposi Verlag is an imprint of Outlook Verlagsgesellschaft mbH.

Verlag (Publisher): Outlook Verlag GmbH, Zeilweg 44, 60439 Frankfurt, Deutschland
Vertretungsberechtigt (Authorized to represent): E. Roepke, Zeilweg 44, 60439 Frankfurt, Deutschland
Druck (Print): Books on Demand GmbH, In de Tarpen 42, 22848 Norderstedt, Deutschland

ADDRESSES TO THE PEOPLE, No. I.

Counsels on Spiritualism.

BY A

CONNECTICUT PASTOR.

NEW YORK:

PUBLISHED BY M. W. DODD,

506 BROADWAY.

1859.

COUNSELS ON SPIRITUALISM.

And when they shall say unto you, Seek unto them that have familiar spirits and unto wizards that peep and that mutter; should not a people seek unto their God?—Isaiah viii: 19.

The Law of Moses contains the following passages: "There shall not be found among you a consulter with familiar spirits, or a wizard, or a necromancer: for all that do these things are an abomination to the Lord." "And the soul that turneth after such as have familiar spirits, to go a whoring after them, I will even set my face against that soul and will cut him off from among his people."

In accordance with this law, Saul treated sorcery as a capital crime. When his own misconduct became rebellion,—a rebellion which finally extinguished the fortunes of his house in tears and blood,—he was told by Samuel that it was as the sin of witchcraft. It is made one of the greatest virtues of the good king Josiah, that he set a flinty face against all attempts at dealing with spirits; and one of the greatest crimes of the wicked king Manasseh, that he practised and abetted such attempts. Malachi declares that God will be a swift witness against the sorcerer. Under the ministry of Paul at Ephesus, the dealers in curious arts brought their books together and burned them before all men—so great was the felt antagonism between their new principles and their old practice. And even the mild John is found teaching just the same severe Gospel that lighted up the Ephesian market-place with blazing parchments worth fifty thousand pieces of silver; and closes the record with even sterner words than began it —"And the fearful, and the unbelieving, and the abominable, and murderer, and whoremonger, and *sorcerer*, and idolator, and all liars, shall have their part in the lake which burneth with fire and brimstone, which is the second death."

The fact that I find in the Scriptures such representations as these is my chief reason for offering to you some thoughts on what has been called Spiritualism. It is no choice subject. I know of none which I would more willingly avoid. But your attention is now being specially called to it through the press and local circumstances: and, on referring to that Religion whose entire lessons I have undertaken to teach, I find that, so far from shunning the theme, she speaks upon it after a fashion of most free and menacing severity. To her, this invoking of the dead is no innocent diversion. To her, these rappings and questionings at the gate of cloistered spirits are no harmless curiosities with which one can properly amuse his leisure, and while away the tedium of a winter evening. She places sorceries of all sorts under solemn ban. They are such trespasses on the night-side of nature as shall enlist against the trespasser the night-side of God. Whether as principals or accessories, none shall engage in rebuilding that Black

Art which Moses cursed and Christ dismantled, without repeating the experience of Julian, and bringing out against themselves avenging fires from the old foundations. Such are the plain teachings. And, holding them to be divinely true, I feel it my duty to waive objections to an unpleasant and somewhat undignified topic, and for once seek your attention to some explanations and suggestions respecting that system of sorcery which, under the more specious name of Spiritualism, is now ambitiously seeking new credence and incurring old penalties.

A few words will suffice to state the system. In this country, it claims to deal almost exclusively with the spirits of dead men—abroad, it claims to deal also with spirits not of our race. The alleged means of doing this are mostly quite different from those employed in olden times. Then, circles were drawn, drugs burned, rods waved, mystic formulas muttered. Now, tables are manipulated ; a certain fixing of the eye, or certain passes of the hand, induce in persons of a peculiar temperament what seems like sleep or trance ; sometimes, without any visible effort, persons of this class fall into convulsions and other strangely-appearing states. It is claimed that, in connection with these things and sometimes without them, wonderful noises, raps, music, motions are observed, when all known natural causes of such phenomena are absent—articles of furniture of all kinds, but especially tables, tip, turn, shuffle about the room, dance about in the air even, and rap out intelligent answers to questions both verbal and mental —the sleeping or trance mediums tell the thoughts of those with whom they are put in communication, detail what is passing in distant places, describe things in the spirit-world—while others, as if their bodies were possessed by other wills and energies than their own, independently speak or write what purport to be messages of Swedenborg, Bacon, Socrates. It is maintained that these are literal facts. It is alleged that, being facts, they must be due to the agency of spirits not embodied. And we are recommended to put ourselves in communication with this agency to learn all manner of secrets belonging to the present and future world—to learn History, Science, Morals, Theology; in a word, almost any thing we choose to inquire about.

Such is the system. No doubt it has many sincere believers. And of course I am very free to admit that there is such a thing as a spirit-world—a world of intelligent, active, and powerful beings not discernible by bodily organs. It is also freely admitted that these spirits—angels, devils, disembodied souls of men—feel a very great interest in human affairs. Not less readily is it admitted that in past ages some of these spirits have actually had with men communications of the most striking character: for do not the Scriptures tell me that angels have visibly brought revelations to men, that deceased Moses and Elias showed themselves to the three disciples on Tabor, and that a large number of persons in the same age were literally taken possession of by demons, who convulsed them, and made them foam at the mouth very much as some mediums are said to do? Further, as a believer in the Scriptures, I fully grant that some of these beings have very extensive dealings of a certain kind with us still: good spirits ministering to them who shall be heirs of salvation; and bad spirits going about seeking whom they may devour, contriving temptations, suggesting evil thoughts, taking away the seed of truth from hearts in which it has been divinely sown. Far be it from me to do otherwise than allow most unreservedly what has had such unwavering reception among practical Christians in all ages! And I may even go so far as to allow that there are some new natural facts lying at the basis of Spiritualism, crude and imperfectly developed as yet, but which in time and in right hands may be of some service to mankind. All this is admitted most freely; and yet I stand here to-day for the purpose of giving a very unfavorable account of Spiritualism, and one as confident as it is unfavorable. I have had my eye on it for years. I have given it such examination as seems to me greatly sufficient. And, as the result, I am bold to testify against it in behalf of both science and religion. To the best of my belief it is their enemy. It is their enemy in principles and works, by stratagem and proclamation, with the right hand and with the left. And the least I feel permitted to say to you is, that it ought to be most decisively, energetically, and summarily rejected; and that he best consults his honor, his safety, and his virtue, who keeps most remote from its influence.

In support of these views I submit the following statements:

I. A vast amount of delusion and imposture has been proved against Spiritualism.

Every person who has been wakeful to the events of the last few years has known very many cases in illustration of this statement. He has perhaps been in personal contact with some; he has known others very surely, only at second hand. They have swarmed to him in the newspapers, he has heard them recited in lectures, he has seen them amassed in books. Mr. Lewis publishes his certificate, Mr. Richmond his, Prof. Page his, Prof. Watson his. Conscious and unconscious muscular action, ventriloquism, concealed machinery, natural magic have all at times been found helping to lift the natural into the supernatural, and expand commonplaces into wonders. Some story bristling with marvels sweeps ambitiously across the stage. After a little comes an annihilating exposure, as bristling with unanswerable signatures and affidavits. Such undeniably has been no small part of the history of Spiritualism. And it has often pressed very sorely the honor and credibility of some of the most prominent promoters of the system. The Davises, the Sunderlands, the Maxwells have ere this found themselves in no enviable position before the public. Their delusions have sometimes looked wonderfully like impostures. Are the two exposures of the medium Fowler already forgotten? Do we not still well remember the birth of the Great Motive Force in Massachusetts? Does not Auburn still blush for the famous colony to Mountain Cove, in Virginia?

The fact is, we need be in no haste to admit all the wonderful stories told of the feats of Spiritualism. Extravagances are no new thing in this field. The history of the system, to say nothing of the intrinsic incredibility of the things alleged, will warrant us in making a very liberal abatement from much that we hear. No doubt we are fairly entitled to suspect that if many of these threatening narratives of facts were properly winnowed of their chaff, the residuum would be neither very dazzling nor abundant. We may fairly presume that a thorough criticism would cut down many of these leviathan marvels to very moderate dimensions.

II. The phenomena of Spiritualism, if granted, have not the least scientific value as proof of its truth—to say nothing of its merit.

By the truth of Spiritualism I mean simply the reality of spirit-intercourse after the manner claimed by Spiritualists. And now I affirm that, to suppose this reality will account for the facts no better than other hypotheses, which on the whole are far less objectionable and hard to credit. Much as I should dislike, both on scientific and religious accounts, to admit in all their length and breadth Mesmerism, Electro-Biology, with hypnotism, clairvoyance and odylic forces ; it is a great deal easier to do this than to admit that such a thing as Spiritualism is true under the government of God. Yes, were I ever to be sorely pressed by the facts, I certainly would deem it, beyond comparison, most rational to take refuge in the dim, wondrous, and interminable caverns of these vaunted sciences. They are the least of the two evils. They leave me my religion. They leave me my faith in Divine Providence. They have a certain amount of plausible basis independent of the facts to be explained ; which Spiritualism has not. And they are able to explain these facts at least as well as Spiritualism can do—especially after some allowance has been made for errors and deceptions known to be rife in the system—if in no other way, at least by showing that there are mysterious depths of strange, yet purely physical and psychological facts, of which the old philosophy never dreamed ; facts as strange as any alleged in connection with the spirits.

Further, as good evidence as exists in support of the

phenomena of Spiritualism, exists to show that they can readily be produced by unbelievers in the system, in *defiance* of spirits, and even for the purpose of disproving the reality of their intercourse; also to prove a thousand known falsehoods and absurdities. I say *as good* evidence: and I speak within bounds. The operator takes his stand, and challenges all spirits far and near. He bids them take notice that he is about to produce the phenomena himself to the confusion of their pet system, and defies them to stop him if they can. He then goes forward, and, in the manner of the mediums, produces the same results as easily and perfectly as the best of them. Or he takes his stand and says, "Listen, all ye spirits! I will produce your phenomena to prove that error is better than truth, and vice better than virtue; that black is white, and the whole of a thing greater than the sum of its parts." Just as successful as before. The tables turn, the raps are given, the speaking or writing trances show themselves—in a word, no believing medium could do the thing better. Now I do not vouch for these accounts: I only say that they come to us as well attested in every particular as any ever put forth by Spiritualists. Are such phenomena as these good for any thing as proof of Spiritualism? What is the evidence worth that is equally good at proving a doctrine and its contrary—equally good at proving Spiritualism and the veriest absurdities that can be mentioned?

III. The origin, means, and modes of Spiritualism are nothing in its favor.

It began about ten years ago, in Hydesville, New York. A family of Foxes were the first professed mediums. If the sworn testimony of a most respectable relative of theirs is worth any thing—if the published certificate of the Professors in the Buffalo Medical College, fortified by the experiments of Dr. Scheff, of Frankfort, Germany, can be relied on, these mediums began their career either wholly or in part as *impostors*.

Also, up to the present time a respectable character has been of little or no consequence to a medium. If his conduct is fair, it is all very well; and if it is as bad as the worst, it is apparently all very well, too. The spirits, even the best-named, do not hesitate—far be it from them to be fastidious! As in the days of Christ, they are glad to enter even into swine. Some of the most efficient mediums are unpresentable in decent society: and at least one is known whose performances were nothing save when he was drunk. And now, behold! by grace of such persons shall tables dance and turn somersaults, pokers and crockery frisk distractedly from floor to ceiling, chairs run tilting at each other, untended violins play dancing voluntaries and Yankee Doodles in the air; to say nothing of scores of other feats equally ridiculous, which this is no place to dwell upon and which yet have a place in the Bibles of Spiritualism. Strange things these to belong to a good system—especially one proposing to teach religion! Strange means, modes, sources! I take it upon me to say that they are no presumptions in favor of the spirits. They are features not very likely to be found worn by a rational, dignified, and useful system. And one can hardly be blamed if he starts back somewhat from the hard-favored stranger as she first approaches him with extended hand, and offers to come into his house and among his precious children, as the high-priest and prophet of a new dispensation.

IV. Spiritualism is rejected by the great mass of intelligent, cultivated, and reliable men who have taken pains to examine its claims—even of those who are disposed to admit as genuine some of the leading phenomena of the system.

Some reject the system on one ground and some on another: but rejected it indisputably is by nearly all the respectability and culture and learning of society. The learned professions, the Colleges, the Scientific Associations, the great Quarterlies of the press, the business men whose faculties have been sharpened and disciplined by the conduct of extensive affairs—you do not find these ranged under the banners of Spiritualism. Spiritualists send a memorial to Congress: it is summarily cast into the limbo of derision and forgetfulness. They ask the favor of the American Association for the Advancement of Science: the assembled science of the country refuse the application without ceremony. They apply to the National Institute of France: that great body gives notice once and again that all papers on that theme will share the fate of those relating to the perpetual motion. There has been no want of due examination of the system by men of this first class. For more than ten years the facts and testimonies, such as they are, belonging to the subject, have been extensively circulated and canvassed. They have been carefully discussed in such periodicals as the *New Englander*, the *North American Review*, the *London Quarterly*, and the *Westminster Review*—they have been probed by such men as make the reputation of the Universities of Edinburgh and Harvard—they have been probed by such men as Babinet, Arago, Faraday, Brewster; also in this country by such as Bancroft, Willis, Bryant,

Cooper, Tuckerman. In a word, the system of Spiritualism as professing to deal with spirits has had abundant investigation from those most capable of judging of its merits—and uniformly with one result. While many have recognized in the phenomena of the system some new and interesting facts in physics and psychology, they all agree in rejecting the system itself as either false or diabolical. I say all. By this I mean that the exceptions are relatively so few as to be of no account: as few, for example, as may be found supporting Mormonism or any other equally preposterous scheme.

This, plainly, is a fact worth being known by persons who have had comparatively limited means of independent judgment of Spiritualism. If, substantially, all the druggists and chemists and physicians in Christendom have certified me that a certain drug is spurious or noxious, I am bound as a reasonable man to have a care how I use it and introduce it into my family. I probably shall refuse to have any thing to do with it—shall recommend the same course to my friends: and who can accuse me of acting irrationally?

V. The ablest friends of Spiritualism substantially confess it worthy of rejection.

This they do by confessing that no dependence can be placed on its communications, and that, granting they are from spirits, the best that can be said of them is that they are largely from wicked spirits, and *may* be entirely from that source. Hear what Edmonds, the leading Spiritualist in this country, says: "In the first place, the mind of the medium influences the message—then the states of the atmosphere and locality have something to do with it—next the harmony or discord of the mortals who are present. And finally, many of the spirits themselves have a very decided propensity to mischief and evil. Selfish, intolerant, malicious, and delighting in human suffering upon earth, they continue the same, for a while at least, in their spirit home : and having in common with others the power of reaching mankind through the newly-developed instrumentality, they use it for the gratification of their predominant propensities, with even less regard than they had on earth for the suffering that they inflict on others. Sometimes it is with a clearly marked purpose of evil, avowed with a hardihood which smacks of the vilest condition of mortal society. Sometimes its fell purposes are most adroitly veiled under a cover of good intentions." Such is the testimony of Edmonds as published several years ago. Within a few months he has delivered a lecture in which he repeats these views in still stronger forms. He says that the mediums often mistake their own thoughts for spirit-messages, that the spirits themselves often make the most egregious mistakes as well as tell the greatest falsehoods knowingly, that wicked spirits often personate those which are good, and that, up to the present time, no sure criterion has been discovered for distinguishing between the two classes—in short, admitting that it is impossible to rely on the accuracy of any of the responses and messages given in the circles till verified in experience.—Hear what Swedenborg himself says, or mediums of the best class in his behalf : "The spirits," says he, "relate things exceedingly fictitious and full of lies. When spirits begin to speak with man, man must beware lest he believe them in any thing, for they say almost any thing ; things are fabricated by them, and they lie ; for if they were permitted to relate what heaven is, and how things are in heaven, they would tell so many lies, and indeed with solemn affirmation, that man would be astonished." —One of the most prominent Spiritualist leaders in the Western States was asked by President Mahan whether he regarded the revelations in the circles as reliable sources of information. He confessed that he did not. "There is not a medium on earth," said he, "whose communications I would commit myself to. If their revelations accord with sound philosophy, I believe them : if not, I disbelieve them." "That is," said a by-stander, "you believe these communications when they accord, and disbelieve them when they do not accord, with *your own* philosophy. Every man must act on the same principle, and we are all left just where we should be in the total absence of all such revelations."

Now I ask such of you as may be invited to give up your faith in the Bible, or any of its doctrines, on the authority of mediums and spirits, to remember these admissions. When you are told that the spirits say that all men are happy as soon as they leave the world, just reply that their own oracles confess that spirits often *lie*, and that there is no known way of distinguishing the truthful from the false. When you are told that the spirits say that the Scriptures abound in errors of doctrine and morality, just reply that their own oracles confess that mediums often mistake their own sentiments for spirit-messages ; and that, if spirits are really speaking, the case is not helped at all—for Spiritualism itself says that spirits are of as uncertain judgment and truthfulness as men. In view of these admissions I marvel at the friends of Spiritualism. If all its information is uncertain till verified by experience, of what use is it? And if every one who goes to the circles is sure of dealing largely with wicked spirits, and *may* deal with none others, why are they not afraid thus to join hands with death and hell? But some one says, "It is the spirit of my father, or mother, or sister, or child, which communicates with me, and I know it too well to fear that it will deceive me." Yes, but the authorities of Spiritualism say that wicked spirits often counterfeit the good: and how do you know that what purports to be your truthful and tender mother is not some Satan in disguise, luring you on to your ruin? You are asked to go to the circles and propose questions to the spirits. Before going, remember that if Spiritualism is true you will go to have dealings, for aught you can tell, with the Devil; and that if Spiritualism is false you will have to answer for your going to that God of the Bible who declares, that he will set his face against every soul that attempts to consult spirits, and cut him off from among his people. And what folly is it for a man to give up the pure and honored and tried religion of his fathers for a novelty that really confesses that there is only one thing certain about it, and that is, that its teachings are largely from wicked and lying spirits! As for myself, I would as soon build a house and stake out a farm on the scarred and heated sides of an active volcano as commit myself to Spiritualism, had I nothing but its own acknowledgments to guide me. What matters it that the smokeless cone to-day shines fairly in the sunlight, and that here and there a blade of green grass can be seen—and perhaps a flower bright as any that ever toyed with zephyr, and nodded gay defiance at the sun? For all this the whole region may be blazing upon me like very Etna before another day has gone.

These ashes still warm to my feet, these furrows newly ploughed by the fiery rivers, these mephitic gases escaping from a hundred fissures, these chasms freshly gaping into hell—God forbid that I should establish my home on a mountain which makes such confessions of its character, and such prophecies of danger!

VI. The teachings of Spiritualism contradict the Bible, the science, the common sense, and the common conscience of mankind—and even themselves.

We have seen that, if the system were true, it would not cast a shadow of suspicion upon the truth of the Bible. Lying spirits are not good witnesses, even against Moses and Christ; and Spiritualism confesses that it has many such, and no means of distinguishing them from others. So all its testimonies against the Bible, if it has such, go for nothing. But, if spirits do actually now communicate with men, the Bible, instead of being discredited, stands confirmed in several important particulars. It is then true, as the Book says, that man has a spiritual nature essentially independent of the body. It is true, as the Book says, that death is not the end of man: there is for him a future state of thinking, active, conscious life. It is true, as the Book says, that unembodied spirits are every where about us, feeling great interest in human affairs, suggesting evil thoughts, deceiving, tempting to sin. Also, the demoniacal possessions of the New Testament are confirmed. Thus a true Spiritualism must furnish a new stone to lay in the already mighty foundation of Christian evidences; just as many an enemy has heretofore done for the city he has assailed. "The Goth seems to be present under the walls, O Belisarius,—bringing stones from far, and building his mounds of attack in the cloudy twilight."

"Ah," says the hero, "is it so? Then to-morrow we shall have the means of strengthening the flanks of the Pincian." And sure enough, the same light that reveals the enemy places his far-fetched blocks in the walls of the city, and Rome is stronger than ever. So will it be on the day that finds the spirits authentic. The Bible shall profit by them. It shall stand all the more firmly on its everlasting hills, through aid of the truths necessarily implied in a genuine spirit-intercourse.

The spirits are no evidence against the Bible; but the Bible is great evidence against the teachings of the spirits. These teachings contradict the Bible: and so all the great arguments which go to show it to be the Word of God—its purity, its reforming power, its adaptation to the entire nature and wants of man, its want of adaptation to serve the purposes of imposture, its triumphant appeal to the intellects and hearts of multitudes of the greatest and best men that ever lived, its prophecies, its miracles established on evidence as massive as supports any historical facts whatever—all these go to show that the contradicting errors of Spiritualism are to be rejected. Now this system has taught such things as the following:—Christ was an impostor. There is no such being as Satan. There is no future punishment. There is no personal God. There is no such thing as sin; and so on to a hundred particulars. I am far from saying that Spiritualism has uniformly taught such things; I only say that it has *often* taught them, and taught them as credibly as it has ever taught any thing—with just as many outlandish wonders, through just as good mediums, from just as well-named and well-behaved spirits. If these messages are unreal or false, there are none in the whole sisterhood of messages which have any thing to stand upon. And that these *are* either unreal or false, I charge in the name of that great mass of evidence that the Bible is true, which for ages has triumphantly sustained the criticisms of the profoundest scholarship and genius, and on which, confessedly, nothing in Spiritualism can cast a shadow of suspicion.

The teachings of Spiritualism also contradict science. And here I hardly know where to begin; for there is scarcely a well-established principle in science which has not, at one time or another, been called in question by the spirits. Does the earth revolve around the sun? What purports to be the spirit of George Washington has no objection to denying the fact. Are the sun, moon and stars placed at unequal distances from the earth? The spirit of Benjamin Franklin makes no difficulty in denying that. Chemistry is a delusion, according to the spirit of Davy; and Euclid mistaken in his theorems, according to the spirit of Newton. I am far from saying that Spiritualism has uniformly taught such things: I only say that such teachings have often been given, and, indeed, can be obtained any day—and that, too, with as much show of astonishing authentication as ever attends on the teachings of Spiritualism. If these spirit messages are unreal or false, pray what evidence have we that any others are better? The rest are no better substantiated than those which so fly in the face of science; and if their evidence is demonstrated to be just good for nothing, just good for nothing is the evidence of all the rest.

The teachings of Spiritualism also contradict the common sense and the common conscience of mankind. I would not have credited some instances that follow, had I not found them resting on authority of the very highest kind. What think you of Bacon, now two hundred years in the spirit world, sending us specimen philosophical essays that would do no credit to a school-boy—of Shakespeare and Corneille sending us specimen comedies and tragedies which their best friends would silently burn, even if dug up in yellow and faded autographs from their old earthly homes—of Clay and Webster sending us specimen speeches, the like of which had they been wont to speak on earth, their public careers would have been of the briefest? What think you of Napoleon and Wellington disputing in the spirit world about their rival tactics, and marshalling over against each other battalions of ghosts in illustration? What think you of spirits operating in railroad stocks? What think you of the doctrine that there is no such thing as sin—that there is no more guilt in perjury, robbery, adultery, murder, than in the movements of a steam engine? What think you of such blasphemies as that Swedenborg went, while in the body, to see the Almighty, and took dinner with Him? What think you of the doctrine that the family institution is a nuisance that ought to be abated, and that the true felicity of mankind is communism and free-love? All this has Spiritualism taught—and much more and worse—such things as cannot be mentioned here for very shame. Now, I do not say that Spiritualism always teaches after this absurd and wicked manner; only that it has often done so, and done so with all the proofs of a genuine spirit-revelation that it ever gives. And, I ask, what is the evidence worth that teaches me that such doctrines are true?

Also, the teaching of Spiritualism contradicts itself. I say but a word here; for I have already incidentally given instances of this species of contradiction. In one circle the spirits will preach infidelity, in another Romanism, in another even Mohammedanism; for an Egyptian spirit even testifies in France to the heaven of Mohammed. You only need to know what sentiments are held in the circle, in order to know what doctrines the spirits will favor. Does such a system as this come from good spirits? Does it come from spirits at all? What is the evidence worth that is equally good at establishing a doctrine and its contrary?

I have sat at the feet of very many teachers; and I am willing to sit at the feet of very many more. But they must have some credentials. I must have some assurance that at least they will not guide me to destruction. In the case of Spiritualism I have no such assurance. Evidently this is no star-crowned angel, beauteous as the blush of morn over Eden, and fresh from the throne of God. She is not even a respectable Gamaliel. Her lessons are often bad, sometimes monstrous, and never to be depended upon; she enforces with the same unction and evidence true and false, good and bad; her flexible needle points all round the compass, and, not seldom, with a profound dip at both ends; she writes her name as freely and legibly on the back of doctrines known by any sound conscience to be shocking and infernal as on others; at times her very breath burns blue, and she thrusts out upon us the forked and hissing tongue of a dragon. Shall we put ourselves to school to such a teacher? Shall we take her into our families to help train our children? Our consciences—shall we give them into her keeping? Our paternal

Bibles—shall we shut them forever for her poor sake, and, with our hands trustingly in hers, go down into the shadows of death and out into the boundlessness of eternity?

VII. Spiritualism refuses to answer certain reasonable test questions, which, if answered well, would prove its truth to most minds beyond controversy.

Christianity gives such evidence of herself as she pleases. And if some one ventures to suggest that certain other proofs would be more convincing to multitudes, she replies that she has given sufficient—that it is inconsistent with her principles to give more. And no one can show it is not so. But it can be shown perfectly in keeping with the genius and habits of Spiritualism to answer such questions as I am about to mention. It purports to answer questions of the same kind every day, and all over the country. Whether relating to matters scientific, literary, financial, political, religious—it evidently is all the same to the spirits. They are consulted about news of the day, about wills, about investments, about dress, about eating and drinking, about domestic matters of the humblest and most secular sorts; and they often find it convenient to give categorical answers on all these topics. In a word, they have the largest liberty of speech—seem embarrassed by few limitations save those of ignorance—are wonderfully complaisant and accommodating to human curiosity. And of course they can pass with the utmost facility every where; no solid bodies are any obstacles to their vision or progress—a few minutes, at the outside, would suffice to carry them down to the centre or round the girth of the globe. They are also represented as very anxious to communicate with living men, and especially with near relatives; also to establish the truth of Spiritualism firmly in the confidence of mankind. How very easy for them to do it! With such ranges of flight and knowledge, and with such large permission to respond about all matters in earth and heaven with which they may happen to be acquainted—how very easy for them to solve certain test questions, and set the public forever at rest as to the reality of their communications! Why not describe those £500 which Prof. Simpson kept so long in bank at Edinburgh waiting their convenience? Will it be claimed that spirits who can pass through granite vaults and iron safes as light through a window, and are as free as air to tell what they can discover, could not do it? Why not report for some paper in New York a synopsis of the news of the *London Times* of the same morning, and do it regularly for a month? Will it be pretended that such spirits as Spiritualism tells us of, would have any difficulty, moral or other, in doing it? On the days that the English, French, Russian and American treaties with China were signed, why could not the spirits have copied them off into the *Spiritual Telegraph*, and called to all the world to take notice if, when the documents came to hand through the ordinary channels, they would not be found the same, word for word? Something of this sort would be very convincing—would shave the now mighty Samson of unbelief of his locks—nay, would strike as many darts through his heart as Joab did through Absalom's: and surely such spirits as Spiritualism tells us of could do it, and would be glad to do it. There are vast treasures of lost gold and gems scattered about the surface of the earth, or a little beneath that surface; there are rich mines of the precious metals, of coal, and other valuable substances everywhere underlying the soil; why will not the spirits prove themselves, help the country, and enrich their mediums and other friends by pointing out the golden spots? It surely cannot be claimed that they lack ability to do it, or permission, or that they are embarrassed with any scruples of conscience! I have often wondered that with such extraordinary and accommodating agents at their beck, the mediums and circles, especially the more needy ones, have not made some discoveries of this sort, and easily lifted themselves and their cause into princely revenues, instead of drudging away at their farming, or fishing, or parish charity. I repeat it, something like this would be very convincing—would clear the atmosphere which Spiritualism now finds it so hard to breathe of its damp, chilling vapors of dissent and dispute, like a searching north wind; and if the system is true, there is nothing to hinder our having such decisive facts. Has anybody ever heard of any thing of the kind? Will any ever hear of it? Instead of retailing such small wares as that some obscure John had a sister married on such a day in Georgia, and so discipling John's wife and children, why do they not, seeing they are as easily able, trade in demonstrations like merchant princes, and so disciple the whole land in magnificent haste? Instead of straying about the country and cutting off his enemies in inglorious detail, in the course of half a century, what general, confident in his star and having the freedom of every method, would not prefer to sweep them away all at once in a decisive battle which should dazzle all lands with his glory, and the echoes of which should dwell forever among men? It is easy enough, and generally safe enough, to give out that a certain obscure woman's husband is dead in California; but let the spirits prove themselves on such facts as we have here mentioned, and which can be verified by every body. Then I, for one, will admit them to be lost spirits, and as such, to be fought against with all manner of truth and righteousness.

VIII. The tendencies of Spiritualism, as historically developed, are most pernicious.

We have seen that the teachings of the system are often of the most immoral and disorganizing nature; and generally so open to mistakes and contradictions as to be just fitted to unsettle faith in every thing. The very *purpose* to deal with what *may* be wicked spirits, is itself corrupting. The results in the history of Spiritualism are just what one would expect. In those communities where it has flourished any length of time, it has weakened domestic ties; fed immorality; gradually passed into spiritual marriages, free-love, Fourierism, no-governmentism, and almost every other bad thing that chooses to take the name of reform. Very recently a colony of Spiritualists started off to found a settlement in one of the Middle States, on principles worse than those of the Mormons. Have you not heard of the Rutland Convention—and do you ever want to hear of another? Such are the results into which the system is continually developing itself; though it has many friends and victims who are not aware of the fact, and would be alarmed and shocked at it if they were. If a Spiritualism with such fruits is true, then, truly enough, Satan is abroad, demoniacal possessions have again come about, the denunciations of the Scriptures against sorcerers and wizards and witches have for us a terrible pertinency; and the sooner we betake ourselves to holy exorcisms of the wicked spirits by prayer, and faith, and good works, and close-clinging to that pure and satisfying Christianity which God and our fathers have bequeathed us, the better.

Such is the system. A vast amount of delusion and imposture has been proved against it. Its phenomena, if granted, have not the least scientific value as proof of its truth—to say nothing of its merits. Its origin, means and modes are nothing in its favor. It is rejected by the great mass of intelligent, cultivated, and reliable men who have taken pains to examine its claims—even of those who are disposed to admit as genuine some of the leading phenomena of the system. Its ablest friends themselves virtually confess it worthy of rejection. Its teachings contradict the Bible, the science, the common sense and common conscience of mankind—also themselves. It refuses to answer certain reasonable test questions which, if well-answered, would prove its truth to most minds beyond controversy. Its tendencies as historically developed, are most pernicious. These are suggestive facts. In their light I trust you have seen the new necromancy and sorcery to be abundantly worthy rejection. So I ask you to reject it for yourselves, for your families, and, as far as your influence extends, for your neighbors and the public at large. Do not practice it, do not consult it, do not patronize it by your presence at its circles. And, to assist your duty, remember the attitude of uncompromising hostility which Christianity, (which Spiritualism can do nothing to discredit), both under the form of the old and of the new dispensation, has always taken toward every sort of an attempt to open up a sensible intercourse with the spirit-world. As we have seen, she sternly charges all who value her favor, desire to maintain a place in her

Church here, and propose to secure a place in her heaven hereafter, to wash their hands of all complicity with such enterprises. We know not all the reasons of her will; but the will itself we do know. It is explicit, decisive, peremptory. It stands out with sharp and angry definition, like that cloud you saw last evening lying motionless in the west—centrally dark, but with its edge sketched on the black sky by the crowded and impatient lightnings in such an abrupt and fiery line as was almost fearful to see. In vain we plead our restless curiosity—in vain, urgent solicitations and the impregnable firmness of our faith. Religion will take no excuse. She has drawn her line, she has built her wall—up to the very stars she has built it; and woe worth the man who attempts, in person or by proxy, under this pretence or under that, to dig through the blazing adamant into the secret things which belong to God.